What do we say...

(A Guide to Islamic Manners)

Noorah Kathryn Abdullah

THE ISLAMIC FOUNDATION

Notes for Parents

What Do We Say... (A Guide to Islamic Manners) is part of the Muslim Children's Library series published by the Islamic Foundation. It is intended for young students of pre-school and primary school age (3-6 years old). At this stage in their lives, the supple minds of children readily assimilate what is imparted to them. This is the right time for them to learn Islamic morals and manners.

The aim of this book is not merely to teach children some standard Islamic supplications (*Du'ā'*) for different occasions; it seeks to instil into their mind and heart the Islamic worldview, the Islamic value system, and above all, the consciousness that whatever they think or do, they should be guided all along by the Islamic teachings. It is designed to make them aware that Allah constantly watches over all human beings and sees whatever they do. This God-consciousness will, *Inshā' Allāh,* make our children better Muslims and better human beings. In this new revised edition we have added the Arabic texts as well.

A selection such as the present one, owing to the obvious constraint of space, can offer only a few illustrations. While every care has been taken to present the most suitable illustrations of the relevant supplications, you are requested to supplement these. As parents your example can be much more effective.

For the benefit of those not fully conversant with the meaning and message of the supplications illustrated, there is a helpful Glossary at the end of the book. Apart from stating the literal meaning of the supplications, it seeks to elucidate their use in given situations. We hope and pray that you find this book useful. We look forward to your comments and suggestions on this and other books which, in your opinion, should be produced for this age group. The sequel to this book is available under the title *What Should We Say* (7-11 years). May Allah reward you for your valuable co-operation in this noble cause of guiding Muslim children along the proper Islamic lines (*Āmīn*).

Editors

What do we say when we begin something?

We say بِسْمِ الله Bismillah (Bis-mil-lah)

What do we say
when we start eating?

We say بِسْمِ الله
Bismillah
(Bis-mil-lah)

What do we say
when we finish eating?

We say الحَمْدُ لله
Al-Hamdulillah
(Al-Ham-du-lil-lah)

What do we say
when we sneeze?

We say الحَمْدُ لله
Al-Hamdulillah
(Al-Ham-du-lil-lah)

What do we say
when we hear someone sneeze?

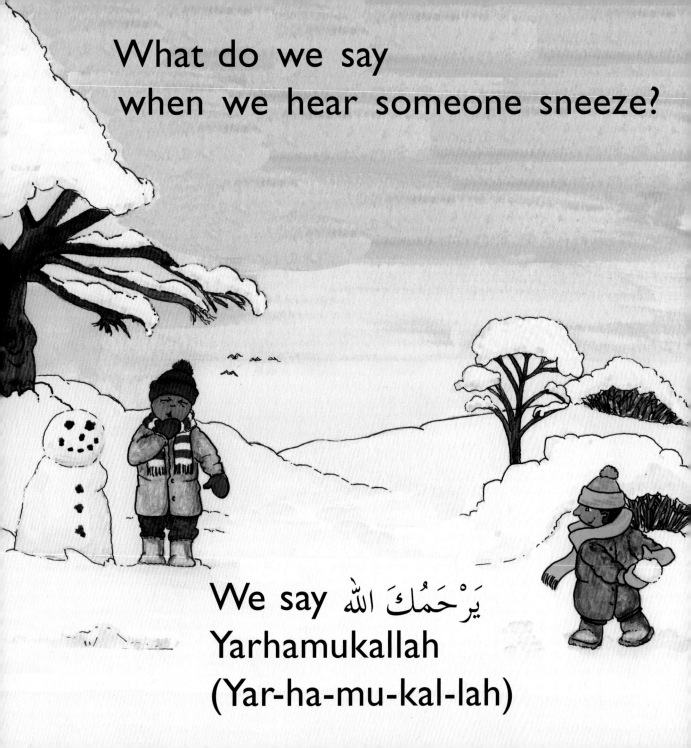

We say يَرْحَمُكَ الله
Yarhamukallah
(Yar-ha-mu-kal-lah)

What do we say when we meet someone?

We say السَّـــلامُ عَلَيْكُم
As-Salamu Alaykum
(As-Sala-mu Alay-kum

What do we say in reply to the greeting?

We say وَعَلَيْكُم السَّلام
Wa Alaykum As-Salam
(Wa Alay-kum As-Salam)

What do we say
when we leave our friend?

We say في أَمَانِ الله
Fi Amanillah
(Fi Ama-nil-lah)

What do we say
when we see something amazing?

We say سُبْحَانَ الله
Subhanallah
(Sub-ha-nal-lah)

What do we say
when we see something beautiful?

We say سُبْحَانَ الله
Subhanallah
(Sub-ha-nal-lah)

What do we say
when we see something nice?

We say مَا شَاءَ الله
Masha Allah
(Ma-Sha-Allah)

What do we say
when we see something we like?

We say مَا شَاءَ الله
Masha Allah
(Ma-Sha-Allah)

What do we say when we want to do something later?

I'll finish it tomorrow!

We say إِن شَاءَ الله Insha Allah (In-Sha-Allah)

What do we say
when we plan something?

We say إِن شَاءَ الله
Insha Allah
(In-Sha-Allah)

What do we say when we lose something?

We say إِنَّا لله
Innalillah
(In-na-lil-lah)

What do we say
when we do something bad?

We say أَسْتَغْفِرُ الله
Astaghfirullah
(Asta-gh-firul-lah)

What do we say when someone gives us something?

Eid Mubarak عيد مبارك

(For Girls)
We say جَزَاكِ الله
Jazakillah
(Jazaki-Allah)

(For Boys)
We say جَزَاكَ الله
Jazakallah
(Jazaka-Allah)

What do we say when we are frightened?

We say أَعُوذُ بِالله
Auzubillah
(Auzu-bil-lah)